Charm Hall

Mirror Magic

Tabitha Black

Hodder
Children's
Books

A division of Hachette Children's Books

Special thanks to Sue Mongredien

For Holly Powell, with lots of love

Chapter One

"I have some exciting news for you today, girls," Miss Linnet said, smiling around at the students of Charm Hall, who were gathered for assembly. "A very special guest will be dropping in at our school in a couple of weeks."

Paige Hart glanced at her best friends, Summer Kirby and Shannon Carroll. *Who on earth was their headmistress talking about?*

"Now, as you may know, Caitlin Byrne joined us as a pupil in Year Five recently," Miss Linnet continued, "and her mother – Marmalade – is about to begin a world tour next month, but before that, she wants to come here."

Paige's mouth dropped open. Marmalade was only the biggest pop star on the planet right now!

An excited murmur filled the hall and Shannon, who was a massive Marmalade fan, clutched at Paige's arm in excitement. "We've got to try and get her autograph," she hissed. "Whenever it is! And whatever it takes!"

Paige grinned.

"Caitlin, perhaps you'd like to come up here and tell everybody a bit more about the event," Miss Linnet went on. "After all, it's thanks to you that there's such an exciting announcement to make."

Paige and her friends craned their necks as Caitlin, her brown pigtails swinging, bounced on to the stage. She had the same wide-set brown eyes as her mum, Paige thought, but not the mane of auburn hair for which Marmalade was so famous.

The girl waved shyly at everyone. "Hi there," she said. "I'm Caitlin. And my mum was wondering if she could come and do a warm-up show for her world tour right here at the school."

A cheer went up around the hall, and then everyone started talking at once.

"Wow!" Paige exclaimed, her mouth dropping open. "Here at school!"

"Yay!" Shannon shouted, punching the air.

"I can't believe it!" Summer murmured with a stunned grin on her face.

Paige could hardly get her head around it either. Marmalade – the megastar, who went to number one with every new release – was coming to *their* school! She was going to do a concert *just for them!*

"This is *sooo* exciting!" Shannon cried. "Marmalade! We're going to see *Marmalade!*"

"At *school!*" Paige laughed.

Smiling, Miss Linnet clapped her hands for quiet. "Well, I imagine that reaction means you're all happy about Caitlin's news," she laughed. "Thank you, Caitlin, you may sit down again. Now, moving on, I have some teacher announcements, and they are as follows . . ."

Paige tried to pay attention to Miss Linnet but it was hopeless. All she could think about was the Marmalade concert. She imagined Marmalade striding out on to the stage with her long red hair flowing behind her. *I wonder what she'll be wearing,*

Paige thought, remembering some of the elaborate costumes the pop star had worn in her videos. *Will she sing all her hits, or will it be new stuff?* Either way, Paige knew it was going to be amazing.

The rest of the assembly passed in a blur and Paige was jerked out of her daydream as she realized that, around her, the other girls were filing out of the hall.

"I can't *wait* to tell my friends back home," Shannon said as they got to their feet. "They are going to *die* with jealousy, I'm telling you."

Summer laughed. "Same here."

"I am so glad Caitlin's at our school!" Paige added.

"You're not the only one – look!" Shannon said. She pointed ahead to where a gaggle of girls had surrounded Caitlin.

"Your mum is so *cool!*" Paige heard one of them twitter.

"You really look like her," someone else simpered.

"Want to be partners in gym?" another girl asked.

Paige snorted. "Talk about sucking up!" she said. "They're all over her like a rash!"

"And, surprise, surprise, have you spotted who's

right there at the front?" Shannon asked, rolling her eyes. "Abigail Carter, of course."

"I should have guessed," Paige laughed. Abigail Carter was in Year Six – like Paige and her friends – and Paige thought she was the biggest pain in school!

"Your mum is *so* fab," Abigail was gushing to Caitlin. "I'm her biggest fan. And I just love her hair! It's *gorgeous!*"

"Pass the sick bucket," Paige said as they went by.

Summer shook her head in disbelief. "As if Abigail would usually bother with a younger student! What is she like?"

"A nightmare," Shannon replied. "That's what she's like!"

"Well, one thing's for sure," Paige said, as they left the hall – and Caitlin's fan club – behind them. "Caitlin's the most popular girl in school already, and she's only just got here!"

Paige had never actually spoken to Caitlin herself, but guessed it must be pretty hard having such a famous mum and starting at a new school. Paige could imagine how annoying it would be to know that people wanted to be your friend just because of your mum!

Thank goodness my parents aren't famous, she thought suddenly, with a grin. *Otherwise I'd have had Abigail Carter all over me!*

Just then, Shannon grabbed Paige and Summer's hands, and began dragging them both down the corridor.

"What are you doing?" Paige yelped in surprise.

"Come on, quick, up to the dorm!" Shannon said, a mysterious smile on her face. "I've just had the most amazing idea!"

Shannon wouldn't say any more until they were up in the attic bedroom that the three of them shared. Velvet was already there, curled up on the end of Shannon's bed, looking just like any ordinary cat. Paige grinned to herself because she knew very well that Velvet wasn't ordinary at all. The little black kitten that she and her friends looked after as their secret pet had magical powers. Powers which had caused the girls to have all sorts of very special adventures.

"Now, I hate to say it," Shannon said, watching as Summer went over to stroke Velvet, "but Abigail

actually said something I agreed with, w
were downstairs."

"Hang on," Paige said, pretending to choke.
"Can I just go to the window and check for
flying pigs?"

"I know, I know," Shannon laughed. "But Abigail
said that Marmalade's hair is gorgeous and, you
know what, it is!"

Paige watched as Shannon gazed up at the
poster above her bed, which showed Marmalade
singing on stage, her long russet locks shining
under the lights.

"So here's my idea," Shannon said, her eyes
alight with excitement. "Won't it be perfect for the
concert if I dye *my* hair the same colour as
Marmalade's?"

"You're going to dye your hair *orange?*" Summer
asked in surprise.

Shannon rolled her eyes. "Not orange, *auburn,*
Summer!" she corrected. "Won't it look awesome?"

"Well, auburn *is* the best hair colour, of course,"
Paige said jokily, tossing her own auburn curls
over her shoulder. "But dyeing yours – isn't that a
bit drastic?"

...nnon said, flapping a hand as ... suggestion. "It'll be fun!" She ... to the mirror on the wall. "And I ...uit me."

...ollowed her and took a handful of her own hair, then dangled it over Shannon's blonde hair so they could see how it looked.

"There," Shannon said triumphantly, "it looks great!" She glanced over at the poster again. "Marmalade's hair is a bit brighter than yours, Paige, so I'd have to get a different shade, but I think it'll look really cool."

"It does look good," Summer agreed, "but won't it be really expensive to get it done?"

"Not if I do it myself," Shannon replied enthusiastically. "You can buy packets of dye from the chemist. I'm sure it doesn't cost much. My mum does hers all the time." She grinned at her reflection. "And won't Abigail be jealous?" she added cheerfully. "Ooh, I can't wait!"

That Saturday, Paige and her friends went into town on the weekly school shopping trip and their first stop was the chemist.

"'Flame' looks nice," Shannon said, holding up a packet in the hair dye section.

"'Flame'?" Paige echoed, grabbing the packet. "That looks more like 'Satsuma' if you ask me. Shannon, this model's hair is bright orange!"

"*And* it's a permanent dye," Summer pointed out. "You'll get blonde roots coming through as it grows out. Why don't you get one that washes out over time?"

Shannon shrugged. "'Burnished Bronze', then?" she suggested, selecting another packet. "Look, the model on the front of this even *looks* like Marmalade!"

"She does a bit," Paige agreed.

"And it's semi-permanent," Summer added. "So at least you won't be stuck with it for too long, if it goes wrong."

Shannon laughed. "It won't go wrong, Summer!" she said confidently, walking over to the till. "How difficult can it be, anyway?"

As the girls left the shop, they bumped into Abigail.

"I didn't know the chemist sold anything to cure ugly duckling syndrome," Abigail said nastily when she spotted the bag in Shannon's hand.

Shannon sighed deeply. "Firstly, I can only assume you're talking about yourself, Abigail," she retorted, "and, to be honest, you really shouldn't put yourself down like that."

Abigail went very red. "Hey, I—"

"And secondly," Shannon went on smoothly, "the thing I've got in this bag is going to make you totally green with envy. Would you like to see?" Shannon swung the bag in front of Abigail's face, then snatched it away teasingly.

Abigail snorted. "I don't believe in magic potions, Shannon. And it would have to be a miracle potion to make me jealous of *you!*" she replied.

But Paige couldn't help but notice that Abigail's eyes lingered curiously on the bag, as if she was intrigued to know what was inside.

Shannon winked. "You just wait," was all she said.

Back at school the girls went upstairs, and Shannon disappeared into the bathroom to start on her hair. "Fancy going to the outdoor pool for a swim?" Paige asked Summer, looking in her chest of drawers for her swimming costume. It was a warm day, and she felt sticky after all their shopping.

"Definitely," Summer said, grabbing a towel.

They knocked on the bathroom door as they went past and called through to Shannon. "We're going swimming, come and join us when you're bronze!" Paige said.

"Will do," Shannon shouted back, over the hiss of the shower.

Down in the pool, Paige and Summer swam a few lengths before joining in with a water polo game that some of the other girls had started.

"I'm getting wrinkly," Summer said after a while, examining her fingers. "Do you think Shannon's going to show?"

Paige reached for her watch, which lay at the side of the pool, and saw that they had been in the water for almost an hour. "Doesn't look like it," she said. "Come on, let's get out and warm up. I'm *dying* to see her hair anyway." She grinned. "*Dyeing*, get it?"

The girls wrapped towels round themselves and then went upstairs. Paige pushed open the bedroom door expectantly – only to see Shannon standing in front of the mirror, staring at her reflection in dismay. Her eyes were full of tears – and her hair was as orange as a carrot!

Chapter Two

"Oh, no!" Paige cried, clapping a hand to her mouth in shock.

"Well, it's certainly . . . different," Summer said tactfully.

Shannon gave a hollow laugh. "And by 'different' you mean 'awful', right? I know I look stupid!"

Paige went and hugged her friend, feeling terrible for her. "What happened?" she asked.

Shannon's mouth drooped. "I left it on too long," she admitted. "I didn't read the instructions properly. And now I look like this – and everyone's going to laugh their heads off at me!"

"It's not *that* bad," Summer said kindly.

"Lots of people have this colour hair naturally," Paige added, trying to make her friend feel better. "And it will certainly make you stand out in a crowd."

Shannon gave a watery smile. "Come on, be honest. I'm going to have to leave school for ever to have any chance of *not* being a complete laughing stock. I might as well say goodbye to you two and Velvet, and start packing my stuff," she joked.

At the mention of her name, Velvet leaped off the window sill and padded over to the girls. Shannon stroked her, suddenly looking hopeful. "Hey, kitty, you've done some pretty amazing things before," she said in a soft voice. "Any chance you could work some magic on my hair, please?"

Velvet blinked her golden eyes at Shannon, and then began to lick her paw. There was certainly no sign of the shimmering whiskers that usually accompanied Velvet's magic.

Shannon sighed. "I guess not," she replied gloomily.

"Hang on," Summer put in. "Velvet is washing

her paws. Maybe that's her way of telling you to wash your hair! Velvet's always doing clever things like that, and the dye wasn't permanent, was it? It should come out after enough washes!"

Shannon's eyes lit up. "Of course!" she cried, leaping to her feet. "I'll just get the packet and see what it says." She rushed out of the room and came back a few seconds later, clutching the box of hair dye. "Colour will fade within three to six weeks," she read aloud. Then her face fell. "Three to six *weeks*? I can't wait that long!" she groaned.

"Ahh, but remember, that's only if you're washing your hair normally – like every day, or every other day," Paige reminded her, quickly doing the sums in her head. "So, for someone who washed their hair every day, the colour would stay in for forty-two washes. Maximum."

"There you go," Summer put in, "you just need to wash your hair forty-two times. Simple!"

Shannon picked up her towel with a sigh. "Hair wash number one coming up!" she announced, and trudged off towards the bathroom.

Paige sighed. "I've got a feeling that Shannon's going to be spending a lot of time in there over the next few days," she said to Summer.

Summer nodded. "We'd better get some more shampoo!" she said.

"Honestly, it doesn't look that bad," Paige said reassuringly as they headed down to the dining hall for dinner later that evening.

Shannon's mouth was set in an unhappy line. "Yes, it does," she muttered. "Everyone's staring at me!"

Paige bit her lip as they went to queue up for their food. Shannon was right. Everyone *was* staring at her – and it was pretty hard to ignore all the whispering and giggling that was spreading like wildfire through the dining hall. Even Joan the dinner lady seemed to be suppressing a smile as she served them.

Paige and her friends had just sat down with their food when they saw Abigail walking past their table with her friend Mia in tow. Mia's eyes widened as she saw Shannon's hair, but she smiled hastily to try and cover up her initial reaction.

Abigail, of course, didn't bother to hide her amusement, and laughed out loud. "Oh, dear," she said. "Shannon's gone and turned herself into a Wotsit! Is that a hot new look in Shannonland?"

"Just ignore her," Summer said in a low voice, looking down at her plate and beginning to eat.

"Leave her alone!" Paige told Abigail. "I'm sure you have better things to do."

Abigail was smiling, a look of triumph on her face. "Oh, yes, but just tell me one thing: am I supposed to be feeling jealous yet?" she asked.

Shannon raised her eyes from her food to glare at Abigail.

"I guess that's a 'no', then," Abigail smirked before ambling off to her table.

Shannon was very quiet for the rest of dinner, and Paige noticed that not even her friend's favourite dessert, apple crumble, could cheer her up. As the three of them left the dining hall, they passed Caitlin. The younger student smiled at Shannon in a friendly way, but Shannon was so downcast that she didn't even notice.

"Hair dye disaster," Summer explained in a low voice. "She's not being rude."

Caitlin nodded. 'It happened to Mum once, when she left her dye on for too long,' she said confidingly.

17

"Really?" Shannon asked, suddenly perking up. "That's what happened to me!"

Paige grinned. She could see that her friend was pretty chuffed at the thought of having something in common with her hero. Even if it was only a bad hair day!

"Uh-oh, Starkers approaching," Summer whispered.

Paige looked up and her heart sank as she saw Mrs Stark, the maths teacher, walking down the corridor towards them. It was a couple of days later, and the girls were making their way towards the playground for morning break.

"What's that she's got in her hand?" Shannon asked.

"It looks like a cat-carrying box," Summer replied. "We've got one at home just like it!"

Paige got an uneasy feeling as she stared at the box. It was made of blue plastic, and had holes in the side. A horrible thought struck her. "You don't think she's caught Velvet in there, do you?"

"Girls!" Mrs Stark said icily, and she stopped directly in front of them. "I'm looking for a little black cat. I've seen it around the school a lot lately,

18

waltzing along the corridors as if it lives here!" She looked outraged at the idea. "As I am sure you are aware, pets aren't allowed in school, so I'm going to catch it today and take it to an animal shelter. Have you seen it anywhere?"

Animal shelter! Paige thought in horror. *We can't let Mrs Stark take Velvet to an animal shelter! Charm Hall is her home. It has been for* centuries!

"N-No, Mrs Stark," Shannon stammered. "We haven't noticed anything unusual."

Summer and Paige immediately agreed.

Mrs Stark peered at them suspiciously. "Well, I'll keep on looking. I'm allergic to cats, and I really don't like the idea of one having the run of the school," she said. As she carried on along the corridor she called over her shoulder, "Let me know if you do see it anywhere, won't you?"

Not likely! Paige thought, turning to watch the teacher's retreating back. There was no way they were going to let Mrs Stark catch their sweet little kitten. But then, at that precise moment, Paige saw a flash of black fur scampering down the corridor towards Mrs Stark.

The teacher turned back to the girls in delight

19

and then pointed at Velvet in triumph. "There it is!" she exclaimed. "Come here, cat!"

"No, wait!" Shannon called, running after Mrs Stark with Paige and Summer close behind.

"Look, Mrs Stark!" Summer cried desperately as Velvet disappeared into a classroom. "I think the cat went in here!" Paige noticed that she pointed to a completely different classroom, clearly hoping to mislead the maths teacher.

But Mrs Stark ignored her, and walked straight into the room Velvet had entered. The girls chased after her.

"So there you are!" Mrs Stark said, approaching the kitten who was now sitting on the window sill, washing one paw as if she hadn't a care in the world.

"Why don't we just put her outside?" Shannon suggested hopefully. "She might belong to one of the gardening staff, or . . ."

Mrs Stark seemed oblivious to Shannon's words. "Come on, you pest!" she said, picking up Velvet with a disdainful expression. She opened the blue box and put Velvet inside. "There," she said, shutting the lid tightly. "Got you!"

Chapter Three

A sad little *miaow* came from inside the box, and Paige felt tears fill her eyes. The thought of Velvet being sent away was just too awful to bear! "Please, Mrs Stark, please don't take her away," she said, feeling a lump in her throat as she looked at the cat-carrying box. Poor Velvet would be frightened and confused if Mrs Stark took her to an animal rescue place – Charm Hall was Velvet's home.

Mrs Stark ignored her. "Miss Linnet will be pleased when I tell her I've finally rounded up this stray," she said. Then she sneezed. *"Atishoo!"* She picked up the box and strode towards the door.

Paige, Shannon and Summer followed Mrs Stark all the way to the headteacher's office. Miss Linnet was just coming out of the door when they all got there.

"Ah, Miss Linnet," Mrs Stark said. "I've caught that kitten – the one who's been running around the school for the last few months. *Atishoo!*"

Miss Linnet glanced from the cat box to Paige and her friends, and then back to Mrs Stark. "Yes, I've been aware of the kitten," she said, her face unreadable.

"Miss Linnet, *please* don't let Mrs Stark send the kitten away!" Shannon burst out.

"It would be so nice to have a school pet!" Paige put in quickly.

"Yes, that's a great idea," Summer added. "She could be our mascot!"

Miss Linnet held up a hand for silence. "Is the kitten in there?" she asked, indicating the box.

"Yes," Mrs Stark said, lifting the lid. "It's right . . . Oh!" She gave a cry of surprise. "It's gone!" she exclaimed.

Paige felt her heart leap in delight. Clever Velvet had escaped! She leaned over to see for herself. It was true. Velvet had completely vanished. The box was empty!

Well, it was *almost* empty. As Paige stared into the box, she could see a faint, telltale shimmer of gold inside it – a sure sign that Velvet had been working her magic!

Mrs Stark's eyes were bulging with shock. "How did . . . I don't understand. The cat was right there, in this box! Where on earth . . .?" she blustered. She frowned at the girls. "If I find out you three have had anything to do with this, you'll be in big trouble!" she said.

Miss Linnet cleared her throat. "This is clearly a very unusual situation," she said. "Thank you for bringing the matter of the kitten to my attention, Mrs Stark. I'll have to make a decision about just what we should do with it in due course."

Mrs Stark nodded once and walked off, still looking at the cat-carrying box in puzzlement. Paige and her friends immediately hurried up to their bedroom to see if Velvet was there.

"She's here," Paige announced, running over to where the kitten was stretched out asleep on Summer's bed. "Oh, Velvet!" she said, dropping a kiss on the cat's little black head. "We were so worried about you!"

"You'll have to be very careful," Summer said, kneeling beside Velvet and stroking her gently. "You've got to stay away from old Starkers, whatever you do."

"Yes, because there's no way we want her to take you away," Shannon added. "Not ever!"

"So what do you think? Any better today?" Shannon's eyes were hopeful as she waited for Summer and Paige's verdict on her hair. It was the next day, and the girls were in their bedroom, getting ready to go down to breakfast. "Is my hair any less orange, would you say?"

"Um . . . well . . ." Paige said. *What was the most tactful way to say "no, not really"?* "Well, your hair looks very clean," she said in the end, "and the washing is definitely helping, but I guess it'll just take time."

Shannon sighed. "Baseball cap it is then," she said, jamming it firmly over her hair as she gazed at her reflection in the mirror.

"How many washes to go now?" Summer asked.

"Thirty-four," Shannon said gloomily.

Paige picked up her hairbrush. "Have you finished with the mirror, Shan?" she asked. "I've just got to brush my hair before we go."

But Shannon didn't seem to hear Paige. She was intent on busily tucking up the bright tendrils of her hair into the cap. "Maybe if I pull the brim down low like this, it'll hide it more," she muttered to herself. "Or perhaps if I . . ."

"Earth to Shannon," Summer said, picking up her own hairbrush and speaking into it as if it were a microphone. "Your Earthling friends wish to use the mirror now. Please leave the mirror area. Repeat: please leave the mirror area."

"Just a sec, just a sec," Shannon said, still frowning at herself. "I've nearly finished . . ."

"Let's face it, she's going to be there all morning," Paige said cheerfully. Then a thought struck her. "Hey! We could get that old star-shaped mirror out, Summer. Remember the one we found in the cellar last year?"

Summer nodded. "Good idea," she said. "Where is it?"

Paige opened her wardrobe door. "In here. I've been keeping it safe," she said, carefully lifting it out. She and Summer looked it over. It was rather dusty and cracked, and certainly a bit smaller than Paige remembered, but it was good enough to see your reflection in.

"I'll get some tissues to clean it," Summer said, as

26

Paige propped it up on her desk and began to brush her hair.

A mew sounded from behind Paige, and she turned round to see Velvet padding along the floor. The kitten jumped up on to Paige's desk and walked all round the mirror, sniffing at it with her little black nose.

"Hello, Velvet," Paige said, giving her a stroke. "Come to admire yourself, have you?" She returned to brushing her hair as Velvet stared thoughtfully at her reflection in the mirror.

"Here," Summer said, coming back with a handful of tissues. Then suddenly she gasped. "Paige," she said. "Look at Velvet!"

Paige looked down at the little kitten and her heart quickened with excitement. Velvet's whiskers were shimmering a bright golden colour and her tail was whisking back and forth behind her.

"Shannon, quick!" Paige called urgently. "Something magical is about to happen!"

Chapter Four

Shannon rushed over to see what was happening. As she did, a stream of glittering silver sparkles burst out of the mirror into the air. Paige stared in amazement as the sparks swirled around the mirror, making it shimmer with thousands of tiny silver lights. The sparkles wound all around the mirror's frame until they formed a cascading loop of energy, moving slowly at first, but then rushing faster and faster so that the light rippled and blurred around the edge of the frame, like a current of magical silver electricity.

"Wow!" Shannon breathed. "It's beautiful, but what's happening?"

Just as she finished speaking, the silver sparkles suddenly burned so brightly that Paige had to close her eyes. When she opened them again, the sparks had completely vanished.

Prrrrrrr, Velvet rumbled, in a pleased-sounding way, and jumped on to Shannon's bed, where she curled up neatly on the duvet.

"Whoa," Summer said. "What was that all about?"

Paige, Shannon and Summer stepped closer to the mirror. "Look! All the cracks have gone! It's like

new!" Paige exclaimed, gazing at the now-gleaming surface of the glass, and the frame which glimmered with a myriad of colours. "Velvet, that was an impressive bit of spring cleaning!"

"Isn't this pretty?" Summer said, running a finger along the polished frame. "Look, I never noticed all these tiny beads in the frame before!"

Paige gazed at the mirror. Summer was right. Now that the frame was clean she could see that it was inlaid with hundreds – maybe even thousands – of tiny, amber-coloured glass beads. "They must have been covered with dust," Paige said. "They're lovely! What a clever kitty Velvet is."

Summer tickled Velvet under her chin, a thoughtful expression on her face. "The thing is, you never know with Velvet," she said slowly. "Is she just being helpful, or is there something magical about this mirror, do you think?"

Shannon peered at herself in it. "Well, it hasn't made my hair look any different," she said bluntly. "Maybe you could work on that for your next trick, puss?" she joked, stroking the little cat with a grin. "Come on, guys, we'd better go down to breakfast. See you later, Velvet!"

* * *

"Marmalade Fever Hits Charm Hall! Paige Hart investigates," Paige wrote at the top of the page. It was Thursday, a couple of days later, and Paige was up in the dorm, alone. She was trying to come up with a catchy headline for the unwritten article that she was hoping to submit to the school paper, the *Charm Echo*. She read over her words. Then she crossed out "Fever" and wrote "Mania" instead.

"That's better, Paige. Now you just have to write the article," she muttered. She chewed the end of her pen, and tried to think of a starting place but nothing sprang to mind. Paige sighed. She was really keen to write for the *Echo*, but this was her first attempt and it was proving harder than she'd thought. Her friends weren't even around to help – Summer was at gym practice and Shannon was in the computer room, looking up ways to reverse hair dye disasters on the Internet.

When Paige had asked Lucinda, the *Echo* editor, if she could review Marmalade's concert for the newspaper, Lucinda had shaken her head apologetically. "Sorry," she'd said. "I've already got someone covering that."

"How about a run-up piece then?" Paige had suggested. "You know, a sort of countdown to the concert with some insight into how people are feeling about it and what kind of preparations are being made?"

Lucinda had nodded. "I love it!" she said. "Brilliant, Paige!"

Yeah, brilliant, Paige thought to herself ruefully. Only it didn't seem so brilliant any more. She just couldn't find the right angle!

Looking up from her notepad, Paige's gaze fell upon the star-shaped mirror above her desk. Suddenly, reflected in its surface, she saw Velvet standing on the window sill behind her, absolutely dripping wet. Through the open window behind the kitten, Paige could see huge storm clouds massing in the sky. She frowned. She hadn't even *heard* the rain; she must have been concentrating too hard!

As Paige watched in the mirror, Velvet shook herself, and drops of water flew everywhere. Paige grinned and got up from her desk to find a towel she could use to dry the kitten. But then she stopped in confusion, because Velvet wasn't on the window sill, she was asleep on Summer's bed. And it wasn't even raining. When Paige looked outside, the sky was blue and the gardens looked completely dry!

But I just saw rain clouds in the mirror, Paige thought, whirling back to look again, but now the beautiful old looking glass reflected only Paige's surprised face, with the window and the blue sky behind.

"Weird!" Paige said aloud.

A little mew came from behind her, and Paige turned to see Velvet trotting along Summer's bed. Paige stroked her, feeling rattled. "I must have been working too hard," she murmured to Velvet. "I've started seeing things now!"

"Talking to yourself?" Shannon asked, coming into the room. "First sign of madness, you know." She tossed her baseball cap on to her bed, looking flushed and upset.

"Are you all right?" Paige asked.

Shannon shook her head crossly. "Starkers caught me wearing my cap, and told me to take it off and leave it up here," she said. "She was prowling the corridors again, looking for Velvet." Shannon bent down and stroked the kitten. "Make sure you stay up here, all right?" she warned her. "We don't want that old dragon catching up with you."

"No way!" Paige agreed.

Shannon let out a huge sigh. "I'm gutted about not being able to wear my cap," she said dolefully. "Everyone will notice my hair again now. And I'm going to get so much stick, I can see it coming." She put her head in her hands. "So that's it. Until it's normal again, I'm just going to have to stay up here and only come out for lessons and food, nothing else."

Paige looked sternly at her friend. "The old Shannon would never hide away like that," she said, trying to give her a boost. "Where's your fighting spirit?"

Shannon shrugged. "Washed down the plughole with the shampoo," she sighed. "It's gone, Paige. Gone!"

A couple of days later Paige was woken by a happy shriek.

"Yes! It's worked at last!" Shannon cried joyfully.

Paige sat bolt upright in bed, to see Shannon

beaming at her reflection in the star-shaped mirror.

"What's all the excitement?" Summer demanded sleepily.

Shannon turned to Paige and Summer, looking ecstatic. "Thank goodness!" she said, grinning. "My hair's looking so much better, isn't it? I can't believe it! It must have faded loads in the night, or something."

Paige rubbed her eyes, looked at Shannon again, and then glanced over at Summer in confusion. In Paige's opinion, Shannon's hair was exactly the same shade as it had been the night before! And judging from Summer's rather bemused expression, she thought the same.

Still, Paige didn't want to spoil her friend's great mood – not when she'd been so miserable lately. "Um . . . yeah," she said in a vague way. "Brilliant news, Shan."

"Come on," Shannon urged. "Get out of bed, you two. It's Saturday, and I want to have some fun. I don't need to hide up here any more – how about a game of tennis after breakfast?"

Without waiting for an answer, she pulled open a cupboard and began rummaging inside for her racquet. Paige sank back on her pillow sleepily – but lurched upright again as Shannon let out a high-pitched wail.

"Nooooooo!"

"What is it?" Paige asked, feeling rather flustered. Shannon was acting really strangely today!

Shannon was staring in horror at her reflection in the ordinary dorm mirror. "But . . . but . . ." she stammered. "My hair is still bright orange!"

Summer looked at Paige in an "is-she-for-real?" kind of way. "Well . . . yes," she said gently. "We know."

"But in the other mirror it looked fine!" Shannon howled. She ran back to the star-shaped mirror and checked again. Her shoulders slumped as she saw how orange her hair was in the reflection. "I don't understand," she said miserably. "I swear it was almost back to normal when I looked in here just a minute ago."

Paige frowned. "Maybe it was the morning light," she suggested, "playing tricks on your eyes or something."

Shannon looked utterly dejected. "Must have been," she agreed tonelessly.

Paige gave the mirror a curious glance as Shannon went to wash her hair for what seemed like the hundredth time that week. Paige couldn't help but think that there was something unusual about the old mirror, but it seemed perfectly normal now. She got up and wandered over to gaze thoughtfully at the looking glass. *What is going on?* she wondered.

Chapter Five

"Could I have your attention, please, girls? I've got an announcement to make – and I think you're all going to be interested." Silence fell at Miss Linnet's words, as everyone looked up from their breakfast.

Miss Linnet doesn't usually make announcements at breakfast, Paige thought with a sudden jolt of excitement, *and certainly not at the weekend!* What could be so important that it couldn't wait until Monday?

"Thank you," Miss Linnet said. "Now, I've just had a call from Marmalade's assistant, Becky."

Shannon dropped her spoon in her cereal bowl,

looking stricken. "Oh, no! Maybe the show's off!" she hissed.

Paige stared at the headteacher with a sinking feeling inside. She really hoped Shannon was wrong. Everyone would be so disappointed if Marmalade cancelled!

"Don't look so alarmed, girls, this is *good* news!" Miss Linnet said, obviously catching sight of the worried faces around her. "Marmalade has requested that, during her performance next Saturday, six Charm Hall students come up on stage with her to dance. Now, if anyone is interested in dancing with Marmalade—"

"Me!" shouted someone.

"I am!" came another excited voice from a table behind Paige. Everyone giggled.

". . . They should report to Miss Mackenzie, who will be holding dance auditions. There will be a meeting about it in the sports hall after lunch today. That's all now. Please continue with your breakfasts." She sat down again, and a storm of chatter broke out across the room.

Paige grinned at her friends. "So, are you guys going to have a go?"

Summer shook her head. "I have a gymnastics exam in a few days. I think that's enough to worry about. How about you, Shannon?"

"To be honest, I'm looking forward to seeing Marmalade in concert so much that I don't want *anything* to spoil it." Shannon wagged her finger at her friends sagely. "Imagine if you were one of the dancers, you'd be nervous all the way through the concert, waiting for your cue, and the whole thing would pass you by! It would be awful."

"I see your point," Paige said, smiling, "and it's not really like we'd stand much of a chance anyway. Not with the likes of Alice Morgan in Year Nine, and Hope Sanderson in Year Eight. They're brilliant dancers."

"True, but not all of the dancers are going to be great," Shannon pointed out. "I bet the auditions will be a laugh!" she added, grinning. "Wouldn't it be fab to be a fly on the wall and watch it all?"

"Definitely," Summer agreed.

An idea had struck Paige at Shannon's words. "Hey! That's a great idea," she said, half to herself. "I could do a news story on the auditions for the *Echo* – you know, speak to some of the girls auditioning and follow their progress. There might be some really dramatic stories in there. I could follow the triumphs and the failures, the drama and the tears. It's perfect!"

Shannon nodded. "I like it, newshound," she said. Finishing her cereal, she sat back in her chair. "So, are we still on for tennis this morning?"

Paige shook her head. "Sorry, I'll have to leave you and Summer to it," she replied. "As soon as breakfast is over, I'm going to find Lucinda and tell her about my idea. In fact," she went on, getting to her feet, "I'm off to scribble some notes right now. See you later!"

"Yes, it's strong!" Lucinda said, when Paige caught up with her in the newspaper office. "You've got the human angle, lots of drama, really big news for the school . . ." She smiled. "Well done, Paige. You could amalgamate it with your first idea about the run-up to the concert. The two would sit well together. And maybe you could interview Caitlin, too, to get her take on it all?"

Paige left the newspaper office walking on air. She glanced out of the window at the nearby tennis courts, wondering if her friends were there so that she could tell them the good news, but there was no sign of them. The sky overhead looked grey, as if it were about to rain. Maybe the rain clouds had changed Shannon and Summer's minds about tennis!

Paige headed to the JCR instead, and popped her head around the door. Her friends weren't there either – but Caitlin was. And for once, she was actually alone, curled up in one of the squashy armchairs, flicking through a magazine.

Excellent, Paige thought, heading over to the younger girl. She could start the interview now, if Caitlin was willing! "Caitlin, I was wondering . . ." she began, but then she broke off at the sound of a loud male voice entering the room.

"Well, if you ask me, the whole thing's a mistake!" the man was complaining. "I can't understand *why* Marmalade wants to do a concert here in this silly little school anyway. I mean, the acoustics are hardly stadium quality, and she's not making a single penny out of it!"

Paige turned to see a man in a black shirt and jeans striding into the common room, with a

42

mousy-haired woman in tow. The man had slicked-back hair and a sulky mouth, and Paige couldn't help but notice that his companion didn't exactly look ecstatic at being in his company. Paige was sure she saw her roll her eyes at Caitlin, who'd stood up at their arrival.

The man and woman came over to where Caitlin was standing, and Paige felt horribly in the way.

"Um . . . sorry, maybe another time," she said to Caitlin awkwardly.

"That's OK," Caitlin replied. "You don't have to leave because of us. You're Shannon's friend, right?"

"Yes," Paige said. "I'm Paige, and I was just going to ask if you'd mind me interviewing you for the school paper."

Caitlin smiled. "That sounds great," she said. "Let me introduce you to my mum's team, as well, while they're here." She turned to the woman. "This is Becky, my mum's assistant," she told Paige politely. "And this is Alec. He's my mum's new manager."

Caitlin was still smiling, but Paige couldn't help noticing the coldness that had slipped into her voice when she introduced Alec.

"Right," Alec said, barely looking in Paige's direction. "Anyway, if this school thing is going ahead—"

"It *is*," Caitlin put in firmly.

"Then we'd better get on with it," Alec said, ignoring Caitlin's interruption. "Becky, get in touch with the crew about setting up the lights and the sound system." Becky hurriedly pulled a notepad out of her bag and began scribbling down his instructions.

"I've also got the list for the final nine tracks that Marmalade will be performing," Alec added, thrusting a piece of paper into Becky's hand. "Thankfully I've got her to remove some of the weaker songs. Now *that* was an uphill struggle!"

Becky glanced down at the list and looked crestfallen for a moment, but then quickly rearranged her features. Paige couldn't help but think that there was something on the list that Marmalade's assistant didn't like.

"Also," Alec barked, "costume changes as above. We'll need a new hair stylist – Toni's still on holiday. And you'd better insist that Marmalade has proper dressing facilities here." He looked around the room disdainfully. "Can't imagine this place will be able to provide the kind of backstage Marmalade is used to, so you'll probably need to work some kind of miracle, but then that's what we pay you for." His phone started ringing. "I've got to get this, then I'm going into town. Catch you later." He marched out of the room without waiting for a

reply, clapping his phone to his ear and barking instructions at someone else.

There was a silence, then Caitlin sighed deeply. "Ugh," she groaned. "Why did Mum ever employ *him*?"

Becky shrugged. "He's efficient," she replied. "He just has absolutely no manners or charm to go with it."

Paige looked over to the JCR door. She really felt as if she were intruding on a private conversation, and Caitlin seemed to have forgotten that she was even there! She cleared her throat. "Caitlin, I—"

Caitlin looked over at her. "Oh, Paige, I'm sorry! You must think we're so rude," she cried. "Let's arrange a time for that interview. How about tomorrow morning at eleven o'clock?"

"Perfect," Paige said happily, jotting it down in her notebook.

"Are you going to be trying out at the dance auditions, Paige?" Becky asked.

Paige shook her head. "I've got two left feet," she confessed with a grin. "I'll be writing, not dancing."

"Hey, I've just thought," Caitlin said. "You should interview Becky too. She's the one organizing the whole thing." She laughed. "Well, actually, Alec *thinks* that he's organizing it, obviously, but we all know it's Becky who ends up doing everything." She looked thoughtful. "It's a shame I can't get Mum to have a word with you too, Paige, but she's so wrapped up in the world tour, she can't think of anything else right now." Her expression became wistful. "We were meant to be going to Brownsea Island to see the red squirrels together," she added, "but she's too busy for that now."

Becky put a comforting arm around Caitlin. "It's not your mum's fault," she said. "Alec has set out a really punishing schedule for her that's taking up all her time." She turned to Paige. "And I'm happy to be interviewed for your piece, Paige," she said. "I'll be at the auditions on Monday, so maybe we could catch up then?"

Paige smiled. This was going better than she ever could have hoped! "Thank you," she said. "That's great!"

Paige all but danced up to the dorm, she was

feeling so pleased with the way things had gone. An interview with Caitlin *and* Marmalade's assistant in her piece would be such a result! Not bad going for her first article. She hoped Shannon and Summer would be upstairs. She couldn't wait to tell them!

Paige pushed open the bedroom door, but the room was empty. Where were her friends? Paige looked out of the window and saw that it was now pouring with rain. Surely Shannon and Summer weren't still playing tennis?

At that instant Paige saw Velvet slip through the open window on to the window sill, her black fur wet and bedraggled. She shook herself, and raindrops flew everywhere.

Paige gasped as a strong sense of déjà vu swept over her. Paige had seen this exact scene before – two days ago, in the star-shaped mirror!

Chapter Six

Paige was just drying Velvet with an old towel when she heard the door open behind her. She turned to see Summer and Shannon walking in.

"Are you all right?" Summer asked straight away. "You look a bit freaked out."

"I *am* freaked out," Paige replied. "The weirdest thing just happened." She explained to her friends how she'd seen Velvet, soaking wet on the window sill, and how she'd seen *exactly* the same thing in the mirror two days earlier. She bit her lip as she finished speaking. "You think I'm nuts, right?" she added, seeing her friends' uncertain faces.

"Err . . ." Summer began, but Shannon interrupted.

"You know, I think there *is* something a bit strange about that mirror," she said. "Remember this morning, when I thought I saw myself with normal hair? Well, I'm *sure* that wasn't just a trick of the light. The mirror definitely showed my hair looking blonde."

Paige nodded. "And I know what I saw in the mirror too," she said. She glanced down at Velvet, feeling a rush of excitement. "So do you think it means the mirror might be . . . magical? Maybe it shows us things that we really want to see?"

Shannon's eyes lit up. "Oooh, a magic mirror, yes!" she said eagerly, running over to look into it. "Come on, mirror, show me something miraculous!" she ordered.

Summer and Paige went over too, but the mirror only showed their three enquiring faces, and nothing more. All the same, Paige felt certain she had hit on something. Why had Velvet worked her magic on the star-shaped mirror? What kind of magic was it? And what was it going to reveal next?

* * *

After lunch Paige took her notepad and pen along to the dance audition meeting that was being held in the sports hall. She was really excited about her article. She just hoped that it came together. Shannon and Summer had stayed in the dorm with the mirror, to check that it didn't show anything strange again.

Paige pushed open the door of the sports hall to find it absolutely packed with girls, all gazing expectantly at the far end of the room where Miss Mackenzie and Becky were standing.

"Hello, everyone," Miss Mackenzie said, as Paige slipped into a seat at the back of the hall and flipped open her notepad. "What a turn-out! It's wonderful to see so many of you here. This is Becky, Marmalade's personal assistant. She will be overseeing the auditions with me. Becky, would you like to say a few words to the girls?"

Becky smiled at the audience. "Hello, there," she said. "As you might know, Marmalade would like six of you to dance on stage with her for the closing song of the concert, 'Tell Me Twice'."

There was an excited murmur from the audience, and Paige overheard one Year Seven girl say, "I *love* that song!"

"We'll be holding the auditions on Monday," Becky continued, "and we'd like you to prepare a two-minute routine to a song of your choice. It doesn't have to be a routine for 'Tell Me Twice', it can be anything that shows off your dancing skills."

"Thanks, Becky," Miss Mackenzie said. "Now remember, girls, this is supposed to be fun, so don't take it too seriously and please don't be too disappointed if you're not picked on Monday. You're all going to have a great time at the concert, whether you're dancing on stage or watching from the audience."

"If anyone has any questions, I'll be here for a little while, so feel free to come and ask me," Becky added. "Otherwise we'll see you on Monday!"

There was a scrape of chairs as everyone got to their feet. Some seemed keen to get practising right away, Paige noticed, while others hung around talking in small groups.

"I know *just* the song," one girl declared to her friend as they raced past Paige.

"This is so exciting!" another girl was saying to her mates. "But what are we going to *wear*?"

Paige scanned the room and saw Melanie Adams, one of her classmates. "Mel, have you got a minute?" she asked. "I'm covering the auditions for the *Echo*. Are you going to be trying out?"

"Too right I am!" Melanie replied enthusiastically.

Paige smiled. "Great. Could I interview you on how you're feeling about the whole thing?"

"Sure," Melanie said with a grin. "And I can tell you what song I'm going to use for my dance routine too!"

Six mini-interviews later, Paige was feeling pleased with her work. Two of the girls she'd talked to were best friends, and were planning to dance a routine together. One was a budding ballerina who wanted to try something completely different. Another was incredibly shy, but a huge Marmalade fan, and the fifth was super-confident that she'd get picked to dance in the show. She'd even done some wild dancing on the spot while Paige was interviewing her.

Paige sat down on one of the chairs and quickly jotted down some notes. There were only a few girls left in the room now, including Caitlin and a couple of her friends. Abigail Carter was there as well, sucking up to Caitlin as usual.

"What do you think your mum will be looking for at the auditions, Cait?" Paige heard Abigail ask.

"It's Cait*lin*," Caitlin replied, a little shortly, and Paige guessed that she wasn't all that interested in having Abigail as her one-girl fan club. "And my mum won't *be* at the auditions. It'll just be Becky and Miss Mackenzie who decide."

"And er . . ." Abigail gave a huge smile. "Will *you* have any say in who gets picked, Caitlin?"

Paige had to try hard not to groan out loud at the question. Abigail was clearly trying to butter up Caitlin in the hope that it would get her a place on stage. *Trust Abigail!* Paige thought.

Just then Caitlin glanced over, spotted Paige and promptly gave her an imploring look, as if to say, "Rescue me!"

Paige took the hint and walked over. "I just need to speak to you about our interview tomorrow," she said to Caitlin, forestalling Abigail who had just opened her mouth to ask another question. "Have you got a minute?"

"Oh, hi, Paige," Caitlin said gratefully, turning away from Abigail. "Sure. Let's go and chat somewhere more private. See you later, Abigail!"

Out of the corner of her eye Paige saw Abigail scowl as they walked towards the sports hall doors.

"I don't really need to talk to you," Paige told Caitlin quietly as they walked out into the corridor. "You just looked like you needed saving."

Caitlin nodded. "Thanks for the rescue service," she replied. "I was starting to think I'd never get rid of that Abigail!"

"We have that problem all the time," a voice laughed behind them, and Paige turned to see Shannon coming up to join them, with Summer just behind.

"Hi, guys," Caitlin said smiling. "Hey, Shannon, your hair is looking a lot nicer now," she said. "I've got some beads you can thread on to the ends if you like. They'll make your hair look really funky."

Shannon looked delighted. "Cheers — that sounds great," she said. "Maybe you could come up to our room. We're in Lilac Dorm in the attic."

"Sure," Caitlin said. "That would be cool. See you all later!"

That evening, as Paige, Summer and Shannon got ready for bed, Shannon kept admiring herself in the star-shaped mirror. Caitlin had brought a box of beads and coloured threads up to their dorm that afternoon, and shown them how to do hair wraps. She'd tied the embroidery threads round and round a section of hair, then fastened it with beads at the bottom.

"I bet Starkers will have a fit and get us to take them out, but they *do* look fab," Shannon said, swinging her head from side to side, so that her silver and blue beads tinkled merrily.

"Caitlin's really nice, isn't she?" Paige commented, playing with one of her own plaits that Caitlin had done in aquamarine and emerald threads. "And she seems so *normal*, which is amazing when you think what a mad life she must have had so far, jetting all around the world with Marmalade."

Summer smiled. "It does sound as though Caitlin's got to do some really cool things." She moved in front of the star-shaped mirror and started brushing her hair, taking care not to brush out her pink and lilac beads. "I'm really pleased that we got to know her better and—" She stopped talking suddenly and let out a gasp. "Oh!"

"What?" Paige asked.

Summer was white-faced and pointing at the star-shaped mirror. Paige and Shannon rushed round to look, but saw nothing unusual, just their joint reflections.

"What was it?" Shannon asked.

Summer blinked and rubbed her eyes. "I just saw something," she said, looking dazed. "I just saw *myself* in the mirror, in my gym kit, doing a gymnastics exam. I think it must be the exam I am having on Monday. And Miss Mackenzie was there, too, marking me, but . . ." she frowned, ". . . for some reason, Miss Mackenzie was on *crutches!*"

There was a moment's silence. Paige stared at the mirror, trying to make sense of what Summer had seen. "OK, let's look at the facts," she said slowly. "I saw Velvet in the mirror and she was soaking wet. And then it happened for real a couple of days later. Could the mirror be predicting the future?"

The girls all looked at one another. "I don't know," Shannon replied. "But I *do* know that anything can happen when Velvet's around!"

The three girls looked over at Velvet who was lying on Shannon's bed. The kitten just gazed back at them with steady, amber eyes.

"But what's going to happen to Miss Mackenzie? And *when?*" Summer murmured, a worried look on her face.

Chapter Seven

"Phew," Shannon sighed, switching off her hairdryer. It was Monday morning and the girls were getting ready to go down for breakfast. "I'm sick of all this hair care stuff. Three washes every morning, more every evening, blow-drying and brushing . . ." she groaned. "And I had to take out my hair wraps so that I could wash my hair properly. I'd never be a hairdresser. No way!"

Paige smiled over at her. "It seems to be working though," she said. "It really is looking more like your usual colour, Shan. In fact . . ." she went over for a closer look, ". . . I'd say it was golden now. Not quite back to blonde, but definitely getting there."

Summer nodded. "Paige is right," she agreed. "It looks much lighter."

"Do you think so?" Shannon asked excitedly. She ran to the star-shaped mirror and peered into it. "Oh, yes! Golden! It really is, isn't it?" She grinned at her reflection and did a little dance.

Just then Paige noticed that Summer's eyes had grown very wide.

"Guys," Summer said in a shaky voice. "Do you realize that Shannon's hair has gone more or less back to normal *two days after* she saw the same thing in that mirror?"

Paige stared at her friend, her mind racing. Then she nodded. "Velvet was soaked two days after I'd seen that in the mirror too," she added.

Summer bit her lip. "Which means that – if the mirror really does predict the future – Miss Mackenzie will end up on crutches two days from when I saw her in the mirror," she finished.

There was a moment's silence while Paige and her friends all looked at each other, mouths open. "That's today," Paige said quietly.

"We've got to go and warn her!" Summer cried.

"Come on!" Shannon said, running for the door.

The three friends raced downstairs and into the dining hall, where other girls were just starting their breakfast. Paige scanned the staff dining table but Miss Mackenzie wasn't there.

"Maybe she's not in school yet," Shannon pointed out.

"Let's grab some breakfast and then go over to the PE department to look for her," Paige said. "We should have time before our first lesson if we hurry."

The girls snatched up some toast, and then ran across the school grounds towards the PE area.

"I've just had a thought. Miss Mackenzie's going to think it's a bit weird if we turn up and warn her to be careful not to hurt her leg," Shannon pointed out as they raced along.

"We'll just have to tell her we had a bad feeling about her getting hurt," Paige said. She screwed up her face. "It's not great, I know, but we've got to say *something*!"

Panting slightly, Paige, Summer and Shannon arrived at the doors to the gym. As they walked inside, the first person they saw was Miss Mackenzie. She was coming along the corridor towards them – on crutches.

"Oh, no!" Paige groaned. "We're too late!"

"Hello, girls," Miss Mackenzie said, hobbling over. "What are you doing here? Shouldn't you be on your way to lessons?"

"We . . . um . . ." Shannon began hesitantly.

"I just wanted to double-check what time the gymnastics exam is," Summer put in.

"It's eleven o'clock," Miss Mackenzie replied.

"Thanks," Summer said. "Um, miss, are you all right?"

Miss Mackenzie nodded. "I just slipped and twisted my ankle over the weekend," she replied, "but it's nothing serious. I just need to keep my weight off it for a few days. Unfortunately, that's easier said than done. I was late in today because I had to get a taxi, rather than cycling in as I usually do, and the taxi went to the wrong place." She smiled. "But it's not the end of the world. Don't worry. I'll see you later on this morning, Summer."

"Yes, miss," Summer said. "See you at eleven."

The three girls left the PE department and

headed for their first class.

"I feel awful that we couldn't warn her earlier," Summer said in a low voice.

"But until today we didn't know for sure how far into the future the mirror predicts," Paige reminded her.

"We know now though," Shannon said. "The star-shaped mirror is *definitely* showing us glimpses of the future. Glimpses of things that will happen around two days later!"

Paige couldn't stop thinking about the mirror all day after that. She and her friends kept running upstairs to peep into the mirror between lessons, hoping to see something special, but nothing unusual happened. They did get some news that day, though: Summer passed her gymnastics exam with flying colours.

After lessons had finished for the day, Paige went up to the dorm to grab her exercise book and pen before the dance auditions started. Summer and Shannon had already gone down to the sports hall to help set up and Paige was really looking forward to watching the auditions. She'd had a

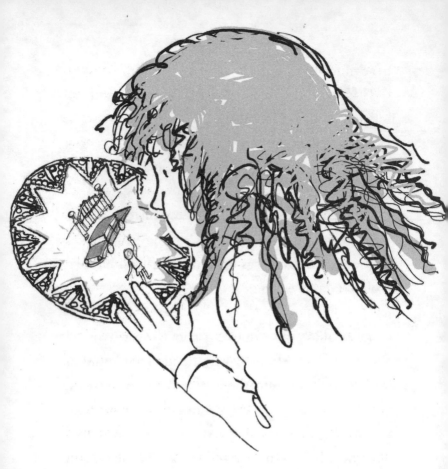

great interview with Caitlin on Sunday and she was
certain there'd be a few good stories to come out of
the try-outs.

Inside the dorm Paige picked up her things and
glanced at the star-shaped mirror as she turned to
go, but then she stopped dead as a new scene
unfolded before her eyes.

64

In the mirror, she could see Caitlin standing outside the front of the school. A black car drew up outside and Caitlin waved at someone inside it before running over and climbing into the back seat. A few seconds later the car sped away from the school – and then the scene faded, and all Paige could see was her own puzzled face gazing back at her.

Paige frowned. *What was that all about?* she wondered. *So Caitlin will be leaving school in a black car two days from now, but why did the mirror show me that?*

Paige stared at the mirror, deep in thought. How she wished the star-shaped mirror had a rewind button. She wanted to see the scene again, and check to see if she'd missed anything significant.

"Where was Caitlin going?" she murmured aloud to the mirror. "And why is it important enough to show me anyway?"

Chapter Eight

The sports hall was a hive of activity, with what looked like half the school filling the enormous room. Paige spotted Shannon and Summer in one corner by the speakers and raced over to them.

"We're having a nightmare," Shannon growled as Paige arrived. "More than forty girls are trying out, which means there are forty songs to get in the right order. And as if that wasn't bad enough, loads of people have left their CDs here without names on, and—"

"I've just seen something in the mirror!" Paige interrupted. "But I don't know what it means."

Shannon stopped at once. "What?" she asked.

"What was it?" Summer demanded at the same time.

Paige described the events she'd seen in the mirror, and the three of them fell silent.

"I feel like the mirror must be showing us these things for a reason," Summer said thoughtfully. "But—"

"Girls? How are you getting on?" called Miss Mackenzie's voice from across the hall. "Are you nearly ready?"

"Nearly!" Shannon called back.

"Sorry, Paige, we've got to get on," Summer said. "But we'll keep thinking about it, and hopefully one of us will work it out."

"Sure," Paige replied. "See you in a bit."

She sat down at the back of the hall and opened her notebook to jot down a few ideas about the pre-audition atmosphere. There were rows and rows of chairs set out in the hall for people who had come to watch. Becky and Miss Mackenzie had seats at the front, with a table which was covered with papers. An excited buzz of voices filled the room, broken by a few nervous giggles every now and then.

67

Some of the girls who were trying out had really gone to town on their outfits. One had a bright-pink catsuit and pigtails, with fluffy pink scrunchies. Another was in a ballet tutu and ballet shoes. Someone else was in a red leotard and tap shoes.

A few minutes later Miss Mackenzie stood up and everyone fell quiet. "Welcome, girls. Now, you should all have been given a number," she said. "Is there anyone here who doesn't have one?" There was silence, and she smiled. "Good," she said. "Then let's have number one up here, please – Jessica Gray, I believe – and we can begin!"

A girl wearing a sticker with the number "1" on it came up to the front. She was older than Paige and simply dressed in her PE kit and bare feet. She stood in the centre of the stage area waiting calmly to begin. Then on came her music, with a thumping bass line and a catchy melody, and she began to dance.

Wow! thought Paige, because Jessica seemed to have come alive with the music, her arms and legs moving in perfect rhythm. She leaped and spun around the sports hall floor with energy and grace. It made Paige smile just to watch. "Jessica Gray started the auditions with a bang – she definitely had the wow factor," she scribbled in her notebook. "A great performance!"

As the music faded away, everyone clapped, and Jessica did a little bow before slipping back to her seat.

Unfortunately, not every dancer was as good as Jessica. One girl, Maisie, had terrible stage fright, and absolutely froze when it was her turn to perform. Paige watched sympathetically as she eventually dashed out of the hall, saying that she'd changed her mind.

Another girl called Anna was doing a set of high kicks when her tights split with a loud *rrrrrip!* Amazingly she barely faltered, just blushed a little and carried on dancing. Paige was impressed. "Anna was a true performer," she wrote, "because she kept going despite knowing that half the audience could see her knickers!"

Melanie, the girl in Paige's form group, was good too, as were the two girls she'd interviewed who had chosen to do their dance routine together. Then it was Abigail's turn, and Paige tried to keep a straight face as Abigail strutted to the

front in silver tap shoes, a silver leotard and a silver
top hat. She put on a showgirl-type performance,
but, unfortunately for Abigail, although her outfit

was dazzling, her dance routine was not.

Paige had written pages and pages of notes by the end of the auditions. At last, the final girl had performed her audition dance, and Miss Mackenzie and Becky conferred quietly before finally getting to their feet.

"Thank you, girls," Becky said warmly. "You've obviously all put in a lot of hard work for these try-outs, so we won't keep you waiting any longer for our decision."

"As I said before, please don't be too disappointed if your name isn't on our list," Miss Mackenzie said. "Much as Becky and I would love to choose more than six dancers, there wouldn't be much room left on stage for Marmalade if we did."

A couple of people chuckled at this, but most girls looked very tense, Paige noticed.

"Our six dancers are as follows," Becky said. "Jessica Gray, Melanie Adams, Hope Sanderson, Nina Dutton, Alice Morgan and Anna Moore."

Everyone clapped – except for Abigail, Paige noticed, who looked shocked not to have been picked. She stormed out, her tap shoes clattering as she went.

As everyone began to leave the hall Paige managed to grab Melanie for a quick interview.

"I'm just so excited!" Melanie cried, clapping her hands to her cheeks when Paige asked how she was feeling. "I can't believe I'm going to be up on stage with Marmalade! I'm going to learn a dance routine with her and everything. Wow!"

Paige also spoke to Anna, the girl whose tights had ripped.

"Who cares about flashing my knickers? I got the part!" Anna laughed.

Paige grinned and then headed over to Becky. "Hello," she said politely. "Is it still OK for us to have a chat for the school newspaper?"

Becky smiled. "Sure," she said. "What would you like to know?"

Paige and Becky sat down, and Paige ran through a few questions she'd written out in preparation. Becky was really friendly and very chatty and the interview whizzed by.

"OK, last of all I want to ask about Marmalade's team and what the various roles involve," Paige said. "Perhaps we could start with the new manager?"

The smile vanished from Becky's face. "Ah . . ." she said, and then hesitated. She seemed to be thinking carefully about her words. "Alec is a very . . . experienced manager in the music industry," she said in a guarded way. "And I'm sure he's going to make Marmalade even more of a megastar than she already is."

Paige jotted this down, and was about to move on to Becky's own role when Becky began talking again.

"Obviously, different people have their different strengths," she went on. "Our last manager, for example, Emma, was loved by everyone. Whereas Alec . . ." She left the sentence dangling, but there was no need to say any more. Paige got the message loud and clear: nobody was very keen on the new guy!

"If you ask me, Alec is a complete pain in the neck," Caitlin snapped, joining them just then. "He's a control freak who's taken over Mum's life and pushed us out of it." Then she sighed and glanced quickly at Paige. "Please don't print that though. He'd probably find even more ways to cut me off from her – he'll invent a brand-new schedule that'll keep her busy for the next five years, or something!"

Paige gave her a smile. "I won't put that in," she promised. "I won't mention him at all, if you think he won't like it. Shall we talk about the world tour instead?"

Becky nodded. "That would be great."

"DANCE FEVER HITS CHARM HALL!
They moved, they grooved, they strutted their stuff – yes, the dance auditions have taken place for the Marmalade concert, and six talented dancers have now been picked. Paige Hart was there to get the full story . . ."

Paige read through her article in the newspaper office the next day feeling really pleased with the way it had come out. One of the Year Nine girls had been there with a camera, and had taken some brilliant photos to accompany the piece.

It's going to look fab! Paige thought happily, as she left the finished report on Lucinda's desk. *If Lucinda likes it enough to print it!*

"Thanks, Paige," Lucinda said, coming into the

office at that moment. "I'll read it this evening. Are you around tomorrow lunchtime? We could have a chat about it then, if you're free. Just swing by."

"Sure," Paige said. "Tomorrow lunchtime is fine. See you then!"

She hummed cheerfully all the way up to the dorm, and was still smiling as she pushed open the bedroom door. But she stopped humming abruptly when she saw Summer and Shannon's faces.

"What's wrong?" Paige asked, instantly concerned.

"Oh, Paige," Shannon said, "we've just seen something awful in the mirror, about Caitlin."

Paige stopped in her tracks. "What was it?" she asked in alarm.

"Caitlin was sitting in what looked like a hotel room," Summer said. "It definitely wasn't school, anyway, it looked really posh."

"Go on," Paige urged. "What happened?"

Shannon swallowed. "Well, she was watching the TV," she said. "And then a newsflash came on – with a photo of Caitlin on the screen. And underneath, the headline said: 'Breaking News: Pop Star's Daughter Kidnapped'!"

Paige's mouth fell open in shock. "Kidnapped?

Caitlin's going to be kidnapped?" she gasped. "There's no way we can let that happen!"

Chapter Nine

Shannon nodded, a grim expression on her face.

"She wasn't hurt, or tied up or anything," Summer put in quickly, "but she didn't look very happy."

Paige sank down on to her bed, feeling stunned. "What shall we do?" she wondered aloud.

"I don't know," Shannon replied. "Keep an eye on her, I guess. And pile in if we see anything suspicious."

A *miaow* suddenly came from Velvet, almost as if she agreed with Shannon's suggestion, and the girls watched as she jumped on to the desk and stared into the star-shaped mirror, tipping her head to one side.

Something clicked in Paige's mind as she saw Velvet sitting there. "Hey," she said, "do you think the kidnapping has anything to do with the black car I saw in the mirror? Maybe the driver of the car is also the kidnapper!"

Summer nodded. "It could be!" she exclaimed. "Why would the mirror have shown us two scenes about Caitlin if they weren't connected in some way?"

"But Caitlin was *waving* to the person in the black car," Paige remembered suddenly. "She wasn't being dragged off by a stranger. She went over and got into the car quite happily."

The girls fell silent, all thinking hard.

"There's something strange about all this, and I don't fully understand it, but I think one thing is for sure: we mustn't let Caitlin get into any strange cars over the next few days," Shannon said after a moment.

Summer nodded. "Paige, you saw the car in the mirror yesterday, didn't you?" she said. "So that means it should turn up tomorrow."

Paige nodded. "I wish we could warn Caitlin somehow – or Miss Linnet, even," she said. "But who's going to believe us if we say that we saw all this in a magic mirror that can predict the future?"

"No one," Summer replied. "We'll just have to shadow Caitlin all day tomorrow to make sure she doesn't leave school alone, or get into any strange cars. If we make sure one of us is near her all the time, then surely she *can't* get kidnapped."

"But we're in different classes from her," Shannon pointed out.

"I don't think anyone could kidnap her during a lesson," Paige put in. "We'll just have to trail her between classes to make sure she gets to each lesson safely."

Summer nodded. "That's the best we can do," she agreed. "And if we can make sure Caitlin is safe all day tomorrow, then hopefully we'll prevent the kidnap from taking place."

Shannon looked thoughtful. "The only problem is, if the mirror predicts the future, then can we change it?" she pondered. "Maybe it's definitely going to happen and there's nothing we can do to stop it!"

"Or *maybe* we're being shown the kidnap precisely so that we *can* stop it," Summer suggested.

Paige shrugged. "There's no way of knowing for sure," she said. Then she frowned determinedly. "But what we *do* know is that we've got to *try* and stop it if we can."

The next day Paige, Summer and Shannon began "Operation Shadow", as Shannon called it. Paige and Summer both had mobile phones, and even though it was forbidden to carry them during school hours they tucked them into their skirt pockets before they went down to breakfast.

"If we have to split up for any reason, we need to stay in contact," Summer had reasoned. "And I'd rather be told off for having my phone on me than see Caitlin get kidnapped."

"Agreed," Paige said. "Let's go!"

The girls went down to breakfast and Paige immediately spotted Caitlin at a corner table, tucking into some toast. Paige, Summer and Shannon sat down nearby and made sure they finished their breakfast at the same time as Caitlin.

Then they walked behind her to her first lesson of the day.

"That's lucky," Shannon said in a low voice, as Caitlin disappeared into her class. "We're just down the corridor from her for maths, so we can nip straight out when the lesson finishes and follow Caitlin to her next class."

Paige could hardly focus at all during maths. She found that she was constantly glancing at her watch to see how long they had until the lesson ended. She knew that, when the bell rang, they needed to have everything packed away so that they were ready to run out of the classroom and trail Caitlin.

Finally the lesson was over and Paige, Shannon and Summer streaked out of the door and into the corridor. Further down the passage, Caitlin's class was also spilling out of its lesson, and Paige breathed a sigh of relief as she spotted Caitlin laughing about something with another girl.

Once again, Paige and her friends tailed Caitlin to her next lesson, being careful to keep a fair distance behind her, and then doubled back to their own classroom.

"So far, so good," Summer said as they sat down for French. "Caitlin doesn't seem to have noticed us."

Shannon grinned. "I quite fancy myself as a private detective," she said. "There's nothing to it!"

Break time followed French, and Paige, Shannon and Summer made sure they chose a spot outside where they could sit and keep watch over Caitlin, who was sitting on the grass chatting with some friends.

The girls were relieved to see that nothing out of the ordinary happened, and when the bell rang for the last lesson of the morning Paige and her friends sprang to their feet and waited to see which direction Caitlin and her friends would take.

"Looks like they're heading to the science wing," Shannon murmured, as the younger girls headed round to the back of the school.

Keeping a careful distance Paige, Summer and Shannon trailed after Caitlin as she walked through the door, down the main corridor and stopped outside the chemistry lab at the end.

"Uh-oh," Paige groaned. She had just remembered that the science laboratories were kept locked unless a teacher was present, so Caitlin and her classmates would have to wait in the corridor until their chemistry teacher arrived to let them in. And that meant that Paige and her friends would have to wait too; they couldn't risk abandoning Caitlin until they'd seen her safely into the classroom.

Unfortunately the chemistry lab was at the end of one long corridor, so there was nowhere out of sight for the girls to hide. Paige realized that Caitlin was bound to wonder what they were doing hanging out in the science corridor instead of being in their own lesson.

"What do we do now?" Summer muttered.

"Caitlin's coming over!" Shannon whispered urgently. "Quick, let's pretend we're looking at this noticeboard."

"Hi, guys," Caitlin said. She had a curious look on her face. "What are you doing here? You don't have science now, do you?"

"We're ... er ... just reading this," Shannon blurted out, jabbing a finger at one of the posters on the board.

"'PHYSICS FUN! Sign up for Saturday sessions here'," Caitlin read aloud in a dubious voice.

"Yeah, that's me, I love a bit of physics," Shannon gabbled.

"Right," Caitlin said sceptically.

In fact, she was looking so incredulous that Paige thought she'd better try a different excuse. "Actually, we're just hanging out here to kill a few minutes before English starts," she said. "You know what Miss Collins is like, she'll have us cleaning the blackboard for her if we're the first ones there."

"Oh, OK," Caitlin said, but Paige didn't think she looked convinced.

Luckily, the chemistry teacher, Mr Abraham, came along just then, so Caitlin said goodbye and went off with the rest of her class.

"Oh, dear," said Shannon, as Mr Abraham unlocked the lab door and Caitlin's class filed in. "That didn't go very well."

"No," said Paige as the three of them set off for English. "I don't think she believed us at all."

"We'll have to try and be a bit more discreet," Summer vowed. "We mustn't make her suspicious, otherwise she might start asking difficult questions."

"Being a spy is harder work than I thought,"

Shannon said. "But we've just got to keep it up for the rest of the day."

Paige nodded. "There's still time for Caitlin to get kidnapped," she said anxiously.

Chapter Ten

The bell went for lunchtime and the girls rushed out of their English class.

"Guys, I need to go and meet Lucinda to talk about my article," Paige said to Shannon and Summer, once they'd seen Caitlin arrive in the dining hall. "I'll be as quick as I can, but I've got my phone on me, so if anything happens, call me."

"OK," Shannon said. "I hope Lucinda likes the piece."

"Me too," Paige said to herself as she hurried away towards the newspaper office. What if she got there and Lucinda was looking awkward and saying, "Actually, Paige, it's not quite what I was looking for . . ."?

Paige grimaced. *Don't even go there!* she told herself firmly.

She opened the office door and saw Lucinda sitting at her desk. She looked up, with a big smile on her face. "Paige!" she said. "Great article. Perfect!"

Paige stopped still. She could feel a stupid grin spreading across her face. "You liked it?" she asked in delight.

"Liked it? It's *fab!*" Lucinda declared. "Lovely writing style and lots of funny anecdotes. Well done."

Paige couldn't stop beaming. "Thanks, Lucinda!" she said, feeling herself blushing.

"No, thank *you*, Paige," Lucinda laughed. "Thank you very much!"

Paige left the office feeling indescribably happy. She couldn't wait to tell her parents and her friends.

Back in the dining hall, though, Paige soon saw that her best friends *weren't* looking happy. In fact, there was definitely some tension in the air as she joined them.

"Why did you have to do it?" Summer asked, shaking her head at Shannon.

"Yeah, yeah, all right!" Shannon groaned. "I know, it was stupid."

Paige stared at them. "What's going on?" she asked.

"Well, everything *was* going fine," Summer began in a slightly cross voice.

"Until I ruined it," Shannon interjected, looking sheepish.

"Why? What happened? Is Caitlin OK?" Paige asked. She glanced round to check where Caitlin was, and spotted her at a nearby table with some friends.

"We were observing her *discreetly*, like we said we would," Summer explained, "and we were going to sit with her for lunch – but then Shannon sat on her!"

"What? You *sat* on her?" Paige asked in surprise, trying not to laugh at the mental image Summer's words had conjured up. "How did *that* happen?"

Shannon sighed. "I guess I got a bit carried away," she confessed. "I really wanted to sit next to Caitlin, so I could find out what lessons she had for the rest of the day. You know, just to make our lives a little bit easier. So when I saw Caitlin move to sit down, I dived into the chair next to her." She looked down at the table, her cheeks flushing pink. "Unfortunately I accidentally dived into Caitlin's lap! She didn't sit where I thought she was going to."

"Oh, dear!" Paige said, grinning. "And what did she say?"

Shannon's cheeks turned an ever deeper pink. "She looked at me like I was really weird," she mumbled. "And then she suggested that we have lunch together some *other* time. So I guess I should keep my distance for a while."

"Oh, don't worry, Shan," Paige said, feeling bad for her friend. "The main thing is, Caitlin's safe. And—"

Paige stopped mid-sentence because, out of the corner of her eye, she'd just seen a student come up to Caitlin and deliver a message. Caitlin quickly scanned the note and then got to her feet and began walking out of the dining hall.

Paige jumped up. "Caitlin's on the move. I'd better follow her," she said.

"OK, we're coming," Shannon said, standing up as well.

Paige shook her head. "No offence, Shannon, but Caitlin's probably seen enough of you for one day. She might get really suspicious if she sees you following her."

"It's true, Shan," Summer agreed. "We'll stay here and wait for you, Paige. Text us if you need us."

Shannon nodded and sat down again. "Good luck," she said.

Paige raced out of the dining room and tracked Caitlin as stealthily as she could, hanging back behind corners as Caitlin walked along first one corridor, then another. Paige followed Caitlin all the way to the school office, where the younger girl then knocked on the door and went inside.

Paige looked at the closed door and wondered what to do next. *At least while Caitlin's in the office, there's no way she can be getting into a strange black car!* she thought. Paige wandered over to the school noticeboard, absently looking at a poster about football try-outs that Miss Mackenzie was setting up.

Atishoo!

Paige jumped at the sound of a very loud sneeze echoing down the corridor. Then she gasped as she saw Velvet dart past her.

Atishoo! There was another loud sneeze, and then Mrs Stark appeared around the corner, her nose looking very pink, carrying the cat box again. "Have you seen that pesky black kitten?" she asked Paige. "I spotted it just now, but it ran away before I could catch it."

"A kitten?" Paige repeated, trying to look innocent.

"Yes, and don't pretend you don't know the one I'm talking about," Mrs Stark snapped. "I'm determined to get my hands on the wretched little thing!"

"I can't see a cat," Paige said truthfully, gazing up and down the corridor and hoping that Velvet had run a long, long way away by now.

Mrs Stark scowled down her beaky pink nose at Paige. "What are you doing hanging around here anyway?" she asked suspiciously. "You know the rules – you're to go outside after you've had your lunch, not hang around the corridors."

"I just wanted to . . . look at this poster," Paige said, pointing to the football advert.

"Right," said Mrs Stark. "Well, now that you've looked at it, you can run along outside, can't you?"

Paige gave a despairing look at the closed door of the school office. She really needed to keep tabs on Caitlin. She couldn't just leave.

But Mrs Stark looked at Paige sternly. "Outside now!" she said.

Paige sighed. She had no choice. She had to go. She walked reluctantly away from the office, down the corridor and turned the corner. Then she paused and listened to Mrs Stark's footsteps as they receded down the corridor in the opposite direction. As soon as she dared, Paige poked her head around the corner and checked that the coast was clear. Sighing with relief, Paige was just sneaking back towards the office, when she saw Velvet in the corridor again.

Paige knelt down and stroked her. "Neither of us should be here, Velvet," she whispered. "We'll both be in big trouble if we're caught!"

Atishoo!

"Oh, no! There's Mrs Stark again!" Paige

exclaimed. And from the sound of her footsteps Paige could tell that the teacher was just about to turn the corner of the corridor. "She's coming back!" Paige whispered urgently to Velvet.

Paige looked around desperately for somewhere to hide – as there was no way that she could reach the other end of the corridor in time – but there was absolutely nothing that she and Velvet could hide behind.

Atishoo! Mrs Stark was just rounding the corner now. How on earth was Paige going to explain what she was doing back outside the office again?

More importantly, Paige thought with a lurch, *what will happen to Velvet?*

Chapter Eleven

Paige was just about to grab Velvet and try to tuck her into her school cardigan or something – anything to hide her from Mrs Stark – when all of a sudden Velvet's whiskers started to shimmer with a golden light. Paige's heart pounded as she saw the little cat's tail swish back and forth – a sure sign that something magical was going to happen!

The golden shimmer from Velvet's whiskers grew brighter and brighter, until the light extended all around Paige and Velvet.

It's like being in a golden bubble! Paige thought. As the light enveloped her, it gave her a warm

tingly feeling all over, and then, just as suddenly as it had begun, the golden light vanished – and so did Velvet!

Paige felt the little cat's body wind around her legs and looked down, only to realize that her own body had vanished too! Her legs – and the rest of her – were completely invisible! She waggled an arm in front of her face, but she couldn't see it. She grinned as she realized that she was actually *invisible*. As was Velvet. *How amazing is that?* Paige thought delightedly.

She looked up to see Mrs Stark walking briskly up the corridor towards her. Paige felt faint with relief – clever Velvet had hidden them both just in time.

Despite being invisible, Paige pressed herself flat against the wall and kept very still as the teacher walked by. Mrs Stark went right past without seeing Paige at all. *Wow!* Paige thought. *Being invisible definitely has its uses!*

Just then the bell rang for the beginning of afternoon lessons and the door of the school office opened. Caitlin came out and hurried off down the corridor.

Paige followed curiously. *Why is Caitlin going this way?* she wondered. *The classrooms are all in the other direction.* Her heart skipped a beat as she realized that Caitlin was heading for the main entrance of the school.

What if there's a black car waiting outside for her? Paige thought anxiously. She knew that she needed her friends – and fast.

Still speeding after Caitlin, Paige felt in her pockets for her mobile phone and fished it out. She could feel the weight of the phone in her hand, but she couldn't see it. Velvet's magic had made everything invisible. How was she going to get a message to her friends? Paige took a deep breath, she would just have to navigate the phone's keypad using her memory.

Feeling for the roughness of the keys, Paige began texting her friends.

"C LEAVING SCHOOL," she texted, praying that she was hitting the correct keys. "HURRY 2 FRNT DOOR."

Paige pressed send and slipped the phone back into her pocket. Looking up, Paige could see that Caitlin was now just disappearing through the school's big main doors.

Please don't let there be a black car waiting there! Paige thought urgently. *And please let Shannon and Summer come quickly!*

Paige ran after Caitlin and slipped through the doors after her. Then her heart sank, because pulling up in front of the school was a black car — the same one that she'd seen two days ago in the magic mirror!

Caitlin waved at the driver and began to walk towards the car.

"Don't get in the car!" Paige yelled, but Caitlin's steps did not falter and Paige realized that her voice must have vanished along with her body.

Paige felt frantic. What was she going to do? She couldn't just let Caitlin get in the car and be kidnapped! But how could she stop her? And where were Summer and Shannon?

Caitlin opened the car's back door and climbed in. Paige looked around – but there was no one else in sight. Nobody could help Caitlin but her!

Paige suddenly felt something soft and warm wind through her legs. It was Velvet! And at that moment Paige made a snap decision.

"Velvet, you wait here for Shannon and Summer," Paige murmured. "I'm going with Caitlin!" And with that, Paige took a deep breath and dived on to the back seat of the car, just before Caitlin pulled the door shut.

Her mouth felt dry. Her heart thumped. She'd done it now. She'd got in the car with Caitlin's kidnapper! Was *she* going to be held hostage too?

"Had a good morning?" asked a voice from the front seat, and Paige gasped as she saw for the first time who the driver was. It was Becky, Marmalade's personal assistant.

Paige's mind raced as she tried to make sense of everything. Why was *Becky* kidnapping Caitlin? Had the mirror got it wrong? Or had she and her friends misunderstood what they'd seen?

Before Paige could think things through any further, though, she spotted two figures running towards the car, a streak of black fur at their ankles. Summer and Shannon must have got her message and rushed to the rescue, she realized. But then she noticed that Velvet was visible again, and in that same moment Paige felt the warm tingly sensation ripple over her once more. She looked quickly down at her hands and found that she was now fully visible again too.

Caitlin jumped as she saw Paige appear right next to her on the back seat. "Where did you come from?" she asked, but before Paige could even think of coming up with an excuse, Summer and Shannon hurtled in front of the car to block Becky from driving away.

Caitlin's eyes widened. "And what on earth are Summer and Shannon doing out there?" she demanded.

Paige racked her brains, trying to think of an adequate explanation. "Um . . ." she said, floundering, but nothing came to mind except the truth. "We thought you were about to be kidnapped," she blurted. "And we were trying to save you!"

Caitlin snorted. "Kidnapped?" she repeated. "Don't be silly. We're not going anywhere. Becky just wanted to have a quick word with me and drop some things off for the concert. Why are you being so—"

But before Caitlin could finish, there was a click as Becky hit the automatic lock, locking all the car doors simultaneously. She turned round in the driver's seat to look at Caitlin, a strained expression on her face.

"Don't be scared, Caitlin," she said. "I'm just going to take you somewhere for a bit. But you'll be quite safe, I promise."

"*What?*" Caitlin asked, looking completely bemused. "Becky, what's going on?"

But Becky ignored Caitlin's question and turned

back to start the engine and slam the car into reverse. Backing away from Shannon and Summer, she swung the car around in a sharp circle and then sped away down the drive.

Paige could see Summer, Shannon and Velvet chasing after the car, but she knew there was no way they could catch up. She watched sadly as her friends quickly became small dots in the distance. This was it. This was really happening. She and Caitlin were being kidnapped by Becky.

"What are you *doing?*" Caitlin shouted.

"Stop the car and let us out!" Paige demanded.

Becky didn't reply, she merely gunned the engine and drove even faster. They were almost at the end of the school drive now, and Paige's mouth fell open in surprise as she spotted Velvet, sitting on a tree stump at the side of the road. Somehow the kitten had overtaken them. As Paige stared, she was sure she could see Velvet's whiskers shimmering, and her tail flicking back and forth.

CRACK! Everyone in the car jumped at the sound of stone splitting.

"The lions!" Becky screamed suddenly, pointing ahead through the windscreen.

Paige and Caitlin watched in amazement as the two enormous stone lions that sat either side of the school entrance jumped off their pedestals and landed in the middle of the drive with another loud CRACK. Paige narrowed her eyes and saw a golden shimmer surrounding them. This was Velvet's work!

One lion swished his great stone tail behind him, and the other opened his mighty stone jaws to give a thunderous roar.

"I can't stop the car in time!" Becky screamed, slamming on the brakes. "We're going to crash!"

Chapter Twelve

Paige felt Caitlin clutch at her hand in fear, and she shut her eyes waiting for the impact – but it never came. After a moment Paige opened her eyes cautiously and saw that the car had screeched to a halt just centimetres from the lions. All was quiet now, except for the ticking of the engine, and the sound of sobbing coming from the front seat.

Becky had her head in her hands and was crying. Caitlin had buried her face in Paige's shoulder and, as Paige watched, the lions jumped back up on to their pedestals and settled back into being stone lions again, their faces inscrutable.

"I must be going m-m-mad," Becky sobbed. "I'm losing my mind!" She put her arms on the steering wheel and rested her head on them. "First I try and kidnap my boss's daughter and now I'm seeing stone lions come to life!"

Paige thought quickly. "Maybe they were just big cats," she said shrugging. "Big, *grey* cats. They did look a bit like lions, though . . ."

Caitlin sat up, colour surging into her cheeks. "Becky, I don't care about the cats! You could have *killed* us, driving like that," she said furiously. "And where were you going anyway? Why were you trying to kidnap me?"

Becky had tears pouring down her cheeks. She dashed them away and turned off the car engine. "I didn't mean any harm," she said brokenly. "I was just so . . . so upset!"

"Why?" Caitlin asked.

"Because Alec cut my song!" Becky burst out, in floods of tears.

"What song?" Caitlin asked, looking very confused.

"I wrote a song a few months ago, and gave it to Marmalade," Becky sniffed. "I didn't tell her it was

104

mine. I just said it was by a new songwriter. Anyway, Marmalade loved it and said that she would be singing it on her world tour – but then Alec changed all that . . ." Becky gave a long sigh. "He hated the song and said that it was too slow and didn't fit in with Marmalade's image. But *she* liked it! And it means so much to me!"

Paige felt bad for Becky, but she still couldn't quite believe that Marmalade's assistant had been going to kidnap Caitlin, just because of a song! She felt she must be missing something, and gave Caitlin a quizzical look.

"I think I'm beginning to understand," Caitlin said, with a sympathetic glance at Becky. "Is the song you're talking about to do with goodbyes?"

Becky nodded.

"I remember Mum talking about it. She loved it," Caitlin confirmed. Then she continued hesitantly. "Becky . . . *your* mum died last year, didn't she? Is the song about her?"

Becky let out a sob and nodded. "I'm so sorry, Caitlin," she sighed. "I wasn't really going to kidnap you. I just thought I'd take you off to a hotel for a bit – until after the school concert."

Caitlin and Paige exchanged glances. "So you were planning to take me away and tell Mum she could only have me back if she sang your song?" Caitlin asked.

Becky bit her lip and nodded again, tears streaming down her face. "I don't know what I was thinking," she said in a small voice. "I must have been mad!"

Caitlin sighed. "You shouldn't have done it, Becky," she said, "but I know what the song meant to you. How about if I talk to Mum, and see if she'll overrule Alec on this one?"

Becky blew her nose and turned to face Caitlin. "Would you? Would you really do that?" she asked.

"Yes," Caitlin said. "I will. But let's go back to school now and forget that any of this ever happened, OK?"

Becky nodded and meekly started the engine. Then she turned the car round and drove back towards the school. Paige glanced over her shoulder at the stone lions one last time, and she couldn't be certain but she thought she saw one of them shake his mane and smile a small smile . . .

* * *

"I'm so excited I think I might explode!" Shannon cried, spinning around. It was a few days later, and Paige and her friends were up in their dorm, getting ready for the Marmalade concert.

Paige was brushing her hair in front of the star-shaped mirror, but she turned to smile at Shannon who had tried on at least six different outfits already, and was now on her seventh.

"Don't explode," Paige said. "You'll miss the show if you do that!" She turned back to the mirror and gasped. "Quick!" she called. "The mirror!"

Shannon and Summer ran over at once to see what was happening. The mirror was showing a picture of Caitlin, Marmalade and Becky on a boat together.

"Marmalade's in our mirror!" Shannon screamed excitedly. "She's actually in our room!"

"Sssh, something's happening," Summer said as the picture changed.

They all watched as the boat arrived at a jetty, and the passengers alighted. They seemed to be laughing as they set off walking into a big, old oak forest. A red squirrel bounded down from a tree, with a nut in its paws, and Paige grinned.

"It's Brownsea Island, I bet!" she said. "That's where Caitlin wanted her mum to take her!"

Summer smiled. "Well, it looks like she'll get her trip after all then," she said happily.

Just then, there was a knock at the door and the images in the mirror vanished.

"Come in," Paige called.

The door opened, and Caitlin came in. "Hi, guys," she said. "I just wanted to let you know that my mum *is* going to sing Becky's song tonight, after all!"

"I can't wait to hear it," Paige said warmly.

"It's great," Caitlin replied. "And my mum always loved it. Anyway, I think she got fed up with Alec trying to make all her decisions for her. She's sacked him and cancelled all her work commitments before the tour, so she can spend some time with me!"

"Cool," Shannon declared. "Have you . . . um . . . got anything special planned?"

Paige could see the eager look in Shannon's eyes, but Caitlin didn't seem to notice. "Actually, Mum says she's going to take me on a trip, but she won't tell me where. It's a surprise," she said excitedly. "I really hope it's Brownsea Island, like we'd planned before!"

Paige, Summer and Shannon exchanged a grin.

"I hope so too!" Paige replied.

"Yes, that would be brilliant," Summer agreed.

Once Paige and Summer were ready for the concert, and Shannon had *finally* settled on her outfit, they went downstairs. Girls were pouring down the staircase, all in their best clothes, talking of nothing else but Marmalade.

"I can't believe she's actually *in our school!*" Shannon kept saying. "This is the best day of my life!"

"Do you think she'll stop and do autographs?" someone else said.

"I can't wait to see her outfits," another girl added.

Everyone was heading for the hall, and Paige spotted Miss Linnet and Mrs Stark in the throng. To Paige's amazement Mrs Stark even had a jolly expression on her face. But just as Paige was looking at her, Mrs Stark suddenly wrinkled her nose and gave an enormous sneeze. *ATISHOO!*

Oh, no, thought Paige. *Velvet must be somewhere around. But where?* She glanced around the lobby hurriedly, only to see Velvet trotting towards her from one of the corridors, her tail swaying and her eyes bright.

Unfortunately Mrs Stark saw her too, and the smile slipped from her face. "That cat!" she cried. "There it is again!" She lunged forward and seized Velvet, holding the kitten at arm's length with a scowl on her face. "Miss Linnet!" she called to the headteacher. "I've got her! I've got the stray! I'll phone the RSPCA right away."

Paige felt sick with despair. She, Summer and Shannon all rushed over to plead for Velvet.

"Miss Linnet, please don't send Velvet away!" Paige cried.

"Yes, please let us keep her," Summer put in.

"She can be our school cat!" Shannon improvised.

Miss Linnet looked from Velvet to the three girls. "'Velvet', did you say?" she asked. She reached out and scooped Velvet from Mrs Stark's arms. "So you've given her a name!" She smiled, and stroked Velvet. "Oh, you're very sweet, Velvet," she

110

said. "But what are we going to do with you?"

"I can drive it to the cat shelter right now, if you want," Mrs Stark put in. *Atishoo!* "Probably best to get rid of it quickly, if you ask me. Someone's bound to adopt it."

Miss Linnet paused, and Paige held her breath. She just couldn't bear it if Velvet had to go!

"I keep seeing this cat everywhere," Miss Linnet chuckled. "I rather think *she* has adopted *us*." She paused, stroking Velvet's soft fur and looking thoughtful. "I'm sure the school can afford to feed one more mouth," she said finally, "especially such a small one!"

Paige stared in delight. "Do you mean . . .?" she blurted.

". . . she can stay?" Summer finished for her.

Miss Linnet smiled. "Yes," she said. "She can stay. It'll be nice to have a school cat, I think."

"Atishoo!" said Mrs Stark, who didn't look at all happy about Miss Linnet's decision.

Miss Linnet looked over at her sympathetically. "We'll have to see if the school nurse can help," she said. "Perhaps some antihistamine tablets would solve the problem."

Velvet gave a great rumbling purr and snuggled into the headteacher's arms.

Paige felt a rush of joy. "Oh, that's wonderful!" she cried. "Thank you!"

Shannon and Summer were beaming too. "Thank you, Miss Linnet," Summer said. "That's great!"

Shannon gave a whoop of excitement. *"Really great!"* she echoed. "Velvet the *school* cat, eh?"

Prrrr! said Velvet happily, and everyone laughed. Well, everyone except Mrs Stark, who had stormed off, still sneezing.

"Enjoy the concert, girls," Miss Linnet said, setting Velvet gently down on the floor. "I'll let Joan know that the kitchen will need to feed Velvet from now on."

"I knew this was the best day of my life," Shannon said happily, as Miss Linnet walked towards the hall. She bent down and picked up Velvet, stroking her lovingly. "We're going to see Marmalade's show now, Velvet, but we'll see you later, all right?"

Velvet purred loudly, and Paige gave her a last stroke as Shannon put her down again.

Paige was feeling very happy as she headed off to the hall, arm in arm with her best friends. Their little magical cat had an official home at last *and* they were about to see the legendary Marmalade live on stage.

And you can't get much better than that! Paige thought with a smile.

**With magic in the air at Charm Hall,
this is one boarding school where
anything can happen !**

Paige can't believe she didn't want to come
to Charm Hall now that she's met Summer
and Shannon, her new best friends.

Then a black kitten mysteriously appears.
She's so cute they don't have the heart to
get rid of her, especially when she turns out
to be more than just an average kitten!

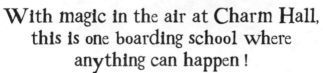

h
Hodder
Children's
Books

A division of Hachette Children's Books

**With magic in the air at Charm Hall,
this is one boarding school where
anything can happen!**

Paige and Shannon think Summer would be
brilliant as Puck in the school's play of
A Midsummer Night's Dream, but she's so shy.
Luckily Velvet, their secret pet kitten,
has a plan that will change all that.

But someone is out to sabotage the play
and the girls are determined to find
out who the culprit is.

Hodder
Children's
Books

A division of Hachette Children's Books

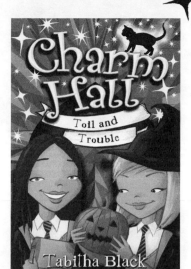

With magic in the air at Charm Hall, this is one boarding school where anything can happen!

A mysterious diary reveals to Paige, Summer and Shannon that a precious sapphire is hidden in the school grounds.

Then they discover someone is trying to steal the jewel! Can the girls – with Velvet's help - stop them in time

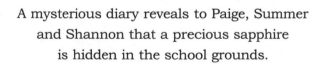

Hodder Children's Books

A division of Hachette Children's Books

With magic in the air at Charm Hall, this is one boarding school where anything can happen!

It's Christmas time and the choir enter a carol competition. But then they find out another school is singing the same carols!

Velvet takes Paige, Summer and Shannon back in time to solve the mystery of why the famous Mona Lisa is smiling and they find a way to save the choir, too.

A division of Hachette Children's Books